Welcome to

Hopscotch Hill School!

In Miss Sparks's class,

you will make friends

with children just like you.

They love school,

and they love to learn!

Keep an eye out for Razzi,

the class pet rabbit.

He may be anywhere!

See if you can spot him

as you read the story.

Welcome!

Student of the Week!

Miss Sparks

Logan

Razzi

Hallie

Skylar

Avery

Spencer

Nathan

Gwen

Lindy

Delaney

Connor

Published by Pleasant Company Publications
Copyright © 2003 by Pleasant Company
For information, address:
Book Editor, Pleasant Company Publications, 8400 Fairway Place,
P.O. Box 620998, Middleton, WI 53562.

Visit our Web site at **americangirl.com**

Printed in China
03 04 05 06 07 08 09 10 C&C 10 9 8 7 6 5 4 3 2 1

Cataloging-in-Publication data available from the Library of Congress

Thank You, Logan!

by Valerie Tripp illustrated by Joy Allen

Logan's Gifts

Splish, splash, splosh!
Logan happily splashed
through muddy puddles
on her way to
Hopscotch Hill School.
She skipped into the classroom.
Logan held up a big, wet bunch
of red and yellow leaves.
"Look, Miss Sparks," said Logan.
"I brought two leaves for everyone."
Miss Sparks said, "Thank you, Logan!
You can hand them out
at Show-and-Tell.
Please rinse them at the sink."
Logan said, "Okey-dokey."

7

Logan went to the sink,

leaving a trail

of muddy drops behind her.

She smiled at the class's pet rabbit.

"Hi, Razzi," Logan said.

"How are you today?"

Razzi wiggled his nose.

Logan laughed. She said,

"I bet in rabbit-talk

that means you are fine.

Do you think everyone

will like the leaves?"

Razzi blinked.

Logan hoped that meant, "Yes!"

Razzi was right.

Logan's classmates loved the leaves.

Logan's Gifts

Funny Spencer stuck his leaves

in his hair like antlers.

Hallie put her leaves together

like butterfly wings.

Miss Sparks wore her leaves

as a corsage.

Logan put the stems in her mouth

so that her leaves

stuck out like whiskers.

She wiggled her nose.

Logan asked, "Who am I?"

"You are Razzi!" said the children.

Then they all put their leaves

in their mouths too.

"No, children," said Miss Sparks.

"That is not a good idea."

Then she smiled. She said,

"Besides, you can't talk

with leaves in your mouth.

And what should we say

to Logan for her gifts?"

All the children said,

"Thank you, Logan!"

They waved their red and

yellow leaves at Logan.

The children looked like trees

waving their branches

in a brisk fall breeze.

Logan smiled and looked at Razzi.

His ears were pointing straight up.

Logan was sure that in rabbit-talk

that meant, "Hurray!"

Logan brought something

for Show-and-Tell

almost every week.

She brought little stones

that had shiny specks in them.

She brought two acorns

joined at the top like bells.

She brought a ladybug

and a squiggly, wiggly worm

that she found in a puddle.

The children wanted to keep

the ladybug and the worm

as classroom pets.

But Miss Sparks said

they would be happier outside.

So Logan let them go.

Logan loved animals and insects.

She would never want to hurt one.

Of course, Razzi was

Logan's most favorite animal.

Some mornings

Razzi was not in his hutch.

He liked to escape.

All the children tried

to be the one to spot Razzi.

Logan was good at finding Razzi.

She knew how to think like a rabbit.

She knew Razzi liked

dark, cozy places.

She found him behind the piano,

under the reading tub,

and inside the dress-up castle.

Whenever Logan found Razzi,

she gave him a kiss on the nose.

Then she put him back in his hutch.

She would say,

"Stay home from now on."

Razzi would twitch his ears

as if to say, "Maybe."

Sniffles and Snuffles

One morning Logan found Razzi

snuggled between books on a shelf.

Logan carefully carried him

back to his hutch.

Miss Sparks said, "Class,

I like the way all of you treat Razzi.

Would you like to help

take care of him?"

"Yes!" said all the children.

They sat up straight and tall.

"Very well," said Miss Sparks.
"You will have partners.
Every week, one set of partners
will care for Razzi.
Now, tell me what must be done
every day to keep Razzi healthy."
Miss Sparks wrote what
the children said.

1. Razzi needs clean water.
2. Razzi needs food.
3. Razzi needs his poops scooped.

The children copied the list

into their journals.

Logan raised her hand. She said,

"Razzi needs love to be happy."

"And hoppy!" added Spencer.

Everyone laughed.

Miss Sparks smiled.

She added to the list:

Logan could not wait for her week

to take care of Razzi.

She gladly helped other children

when it was their turn.

Logan helped Connor take care of Razzi

when Lindy was out sick with a cold.

Logan scooped the poop

for Delaney and Nathan

because they thought the poop was icky.

At last Logan and Spencer's week came.

Logan felt funny on Monday morning,

as if she had a cloud inside her head.

Sniffles and Snuffles

Logan had the sniffles too.

But she was excited

to get to school

to take care of Razzi.

So she just swiped at her nose

and hurried on her way.

Logan got to Miss Sparks's room early.

"Guess what, Razzi?" Logan said.

"It's MY week to take care of you!"

Razzi's ears stood straight up.

He blinked. He wiggled his nose.

"Wow!" laughed Logan.

"You are as happy as I am."

Logan's throat hurt

when she laughed,

but she was too happy to care.

At last Spencer came.

Logan opened the hutch.

Carefully, Logan filled Razzi's water bottle.

Carefully, Spencer filled Razzi's food bowl.

Carefully, Logan scooped Razzi's poops.

When Logan and Spencer were finished,

Logan lifted Razzi into her arms.

She said, "You need love."

Logan gave Razzi a kiss on the nose.

Suddenly her own nose felt strange.

"AH-CHOO!"

Logan surprised herself by sneezing

all over Razzi and Spencer.

"AH-CHOO!" she sneezed again.

They were big, wet, yucky sneezes.

"Hey!" said Spencer. He was surprised.

Razzi was surprised too.

Razzi ducked his head

into the crook of Logan's arm.

"Oops! Sorry, guys!" said Logan.

She gave Razzi another kiss

and put him back in his hutch.

The next day Logan sniffled

as she cleaned the hutch.

Spencer sniffled

as he filled the food bowl.

When Logan gave Razzi

his morning kiss,

Razzi seemed sleepy.

He wiggled his nose only a little bit.

Logan said, "Go back to sleep, Razzi.

We are all tired today."

The next morning

Spencer was out sick with a cold.

When Logan greeted Razzi,

the rabbit just lifted one ear.

His food bowl was still full

from the day before.

Logan noticed that Razzi

had watery eyes and a runny nose.

Then Razzi did

the most surprising thing.

He sneezed!

Suddenly Logan had

a terrible, terrible thought.

"Oh, Razzi," Logan whispered.

"Did I give you my cold

by sneezing at you?"

Logan's eyes filled with watery tears

just like Razzi's.

"Logan," said Miss Sparks.

"What is the matter?"

"Oh, Miss Sparks," Logan said sadly.

"I made Razzi sick!

I sneezed at him,

and now he is sneezing too."

Miss Sparks knelt down.

First she gave Logan a hug.

Then she looked at Razzi.

"Razzi does have a cold,"

said Miss Sparks.

"In rabbits it's called snuffles."

"Oh, no!" wailed Logan.

"My sniffles gave Razzi the snuffles."

"No, dear," said Miss Sparks.

"Rabbits can't catch colds from people."

Logan felt a little better.

Then Miss Sparks said,

"But people can catch colds

from other people."

Logan thought about

all the times she had been

surprised by a sneeze.

"Did I make Spencer sick?"

Logan asked.

"Have I made other children sick too?"

Miss Sparks said, "Several children

in our class have colds.

I'm sure lots of germs

are being passed around.

That's why it's so important

for you to cover your nose and mouth

when you cough or sneeze.

Grab a tissue if you can,

or catch a surprise sneeze

in the crook of your elbow.

Then wash your hands

so you will not give others your germs."

"Will Razzi be all right?" asked Logan.

"Razzi is a good, strong rabbit,"

said Miss Sparks.

"He will go to the veterinarian

later today.

I'm sure he will feel better soon."

Logan's Slogans

What a sad day
for Miss Sparks's class!
Miss Sparks explained
about Razzi's cold.
She reminded the children
that they should be careful
about colds and germs too.
She said, "Use a tissue.
Or catch a surprise sneeze
in the crook of your elbow.
Wash your hands after
you cough or sneeze.
Rabbits can't, but children can."

The principal came to take Razzi

to the veterinarian.

All the children sadly watched Razzi go.

Miss Sparks was sad too.

The sparkles on her glasses

did not glitter as they usually did.

Whenever Logan looked back

at the Nature Corner,

she felt as empty as Razzi's hutch.

"Class," said Miss Sparks,

"do you miss Razzi?"

"Yes," said all the children.

"Shall we make get-well cards for him?"

asked Miss Sparks.

"Yes!" said the children, perking up.

Miss Sparks gave everyone paper.

The children got out their crayons.

Miss Sparks wrote

on the chalkboard:

We miss you, Razzi.

Get well soon.

Logan drew a picture of Razzi.

She copied the words

from the chalkboard

onto her drawing.

Miss Sparks collected the drawings.

"I'll take them to the veterinarian's

after school," she said.

"I'm sure Razzi will like them."

Miss Sparks held up

the drawings.

Logan saw that Skylar

had drawn a rabbit.

Skylar had traced her hands

to make big ears for her rabbit.

Hallie had drawn her own face

with tears coming out of her eyes.

When Logan saw

what her friends had drawn,

she had a brilliant idea.

When all the other boys and girls

left to go to lunch,

Logan stayed in the room.

"Miss Sparks," Logan said.

"I think I know a way

to remind everyone

to be careful about germs.

Will you help me?"

The sparkles on

Miss Sparks's glasses

glittered.

"Of course!"

Miss Sparks said.

After lunch the children came back.

At first they did not notice anything.

Then Skylar said, "Hey, look!"

Everyone looked at Razzi's hutch.

Logan had made three posters.

On each poster

she had written a slogan.

If you think you are going to sneeze
Come and get a tissue please.

People say "thanks"
for leaves, and worms,
But not for icky, sneezy germs.
So please, please, please!
Catch your sneeze.

Using a tissue is a good habit,
says Razzmatazz, our class rabbit.
And do not forget to wash your hands.
Rabbits can't, but children can.

The children were delighted.

They pretended to sneeze

into the crooks of their elbows

or into tissues.

"Who made these posters?" they asked.

Miss Sparks nodded toward Logan.

The children waved their tissues.

They cheered, "Thank you, Logan!"

At first the children

didn't always remember

to be careful about their germs.

But the posters on Razzi's hutch helped.

When Razzi came back a week later,

he was happier and hoppier than ever.

By then the children were very good

about covering their noses and mouths

when they sneezed.

They washed their hands afterward.

They almost always remembered

—thanks to Logan's slogans.

Dear Parents . . .

Leaves, ladybugs, worms . . . and germs! Thanks to Logan, Mother Nature's creations—some great, some small, and some rather dirty—are frequent visitors to Miss Sparks's classroom. Your own young explorer probably has presented you with treasures she has found outdoors, too. A love of nature just seems to come naturally to children, doesn't it? They are fascinated by weather, sticks, stones, plants, bugs, animals, trees, and birds. Mud puddles are irresistible!

Whether your great outdoors is the corner park or your own backyard, you and your child can enjoy exploring nature together. Try some of the activities on the following pages. Don't forget to wear your boots!

The Great Outdoors

You and your young scientist have all the equipment you need for great discoveries: curiosity, your five senses, and each other. Open the door. Step outside. Explore!

• Ask your child to hold up her hand, fingers spread. Tell her that each finger stands for one of the **five senses.** Help your child name the five senses. Next, ask her, "Can you point to what you hear with? Touch with? Taste with? See with? Smell with?" Tell her that she is an explorer and the five senses are her tools, so she'll want to keep them in good shape.

• As you and your child are walking to the bus stop or the mailbox, remind her to **be observant.** Can she find a fallen leaf, a sparkly stone, or a stick shaped like a Y? She can collect and keep these treasures, but remind her to respect nature by taking only what's on the ground—not leaves or twigs directly off trees or bushes.

- Encourage your child to use her five senses year round. Tell her that her window is a **picture frame.** Ask her how the picture of the outdoors looks different in the winter than in the summer, at night versus in the morning. Open the window and ask her what she can feel on her face, hear, smell, or see.

- Explore in all kinds of weather! The next time it rains, put on raingear and go outside with your child. Ask her how the rain feels on her hand? How does it sound? How does it make the pavement look? Does it have a taste? How does it make the earth smell? Let the rainy world be **puddle wonderful** for your child—and for you.

- How does your garden grow? A windowsill is all the space you need for a garden for your child. Put a carrot top in a cup of water and watch the roots grow. Plant sunflower seeds in a large pot and help your child care for them. Watch the **magic of growth** together.

At Home with Animals

Remember that frog your daughter wanted to name and tame? To many children, crawlies aren't creepy, and snakes truly *are* charming! You don't have to have a pet as a member of the family for your child to enjoy the fun of interacting with animals.

- When your child brings home a lovely ladybug or lightning bug, a wiggly worm, or a baby lizard, let her put it in a jar with airholes punched into the lid. Add a bit of dirt, leaves, and a spritz of water. Call the jar the **Cozy Corner Pet Hotel** to remind your child that the visiting creature can stay only for the night. In the morning, wave a cheerful good-bye to the creature when your child sets it free.

- Hold on to those wonderful drawings of animals, birds, and fish that your child makes or cuts out of magazines. See if she can make or find pictures of baby animals to match the grown animals. Talk about how animals **change as they grow,** such as what they look like, what they can do, how they move, what they sound like, and what they need. Remind your child that *she* has changed in those ways, too, and tell her how proud you are of the way she has grown.

• If your family has a pet, let your child be your partner in caring for it. She might like to make a **picture chart** like the one Miss Sparks's class made to remind her of what your pet needs. Your child may not be ready to take on the responsibility of caring for the pet all by herself, but she surely knows—as Logan did—that pets need love to be happy, and that is one need she can help provide.

• When you are outside with your child, help her keep an eye out for **animal homes.** Can she see a nest? A spiderweb? A squirrel hole in a tree? A beehive? A doghouse? A fishpond? Talk about the different homes animals choose or build. Ask which homes your child would like best if *she* were choosing one.

Ah-Choo!

How many millions of times have you reminded your child to use a tissue and wash her hands after she sneezes? Logan's slogans helped the children in Miss Sparks's class remember—at least sometimes! Here are some ways you can remind your child to catch her sneezes and stop them *cold*.

- What is a germ, anyway? Use **fun language** to describe germs: "Germs are tiny creatures that can make us sick. They're so small and sneaky, we can't see them when they enter our bodies. Only scientists looking through microscopes can see them. But we can fight them by using tissues when we sneeze and by washing our hands afterward."

- To help your child understand how germs spread, step outside and put a **pinch of glitter** into her hand, or use a washable marker to make dots on her hand. Shake hands with her to show how easily the glitter or marker spreads. Then have your child wash her hands until the glitter or marker is gone so that she'll see how long it takes to wash off those determined germs!

- Sing a **song of soap suds!** It's hard for children to remember to wash their hands for 15 seconds, as they should. Think of a song your child likes that lasts about that long. Sing it with her while she washes her hands, or make up your own words for a squeaky-clean song.

- Oh, that **tissue issue!** You may already have tissues handy in every room of the house, but they seem to be invisible. Use a drawing your child has made to make an eye-catching cover for the tissue box. Or encourage her to make posters like the ones Logan made for Miss Sparks's class.

- How can you make the importance of sink time really "sink in"? Try the **Before-or-After Quiz.** Ask your child, "Do you wash your hands before or after you eat? Before or after you sneeze? Before or after using the bathroom?" A prize for the right answers might be her own pretty bar of soap.

47

Thank You, Logan! and the activities that follow the story were developed with guidance from the Hopscotch Hill School advisory board:

Dominic Gullo is a professor and the program chair of Early Childhood Education at the University of Wisconsin, Milwaukee. He is a member of the governing board of the National Association for the Education of Young Children, and he is a consultant to school districts across the country in the areas of early childhood education, curriculum, and assessment.

Margaret Jensen has taught beginning reading for 32 years and is currently a math resource teacher in the Madison Metropolitan School District, Wisconsin. She has served on committees for the International Reading Association and the Wisconsin State Reading Association, and has been president of the Madison Area Reading Council. She has presented at workshops and conferences in the areas of reading, writing, and children's literature.

Kim Miller is a school psychologist at Lowell Elementary in Madison, Wisconsin, where she works with children, parents, and teachers to help solve—and prevent—problems related to learning and adjustment to the classroom setting.

Virginia Pickerell has worked with teachers and parents as an educational consultant and counselor within the Madison Metropolitan School District. She has researched and presented workshops on topics such as learning processes, problem solving, and creativity. She is also a former director of Head Start.